Bee & Flea
and the Compost Caper

FOR ZIA —A.H.

FOR ANNIE AND FAYE —M.D.

Text © 2022 Anna Humphrey | Illustrations © 2022 Mike Deas

Owlkids Books acknowledges the financial support of the Canada Council for the Arts, the Ontario Arts Council, the Government of Canada through the Canada Book Fund (CBF) and the Government of Ontario through the Ontario Creates Book Initiative for our publishing activities.

Published in Canada by Owlkids Books Inc., 1 Eglinton Avenue East, Toronto, ON M4P 3A1

Published in the United States by Owlkids Books Inc., 1700 Fourth Street, Berkeley, CA, 94710

Library of Congress Control Number: 2021939198

Library and Archives Canada Cataloguing in Publication

Title: Bee & Flea, and the compost caper / written by Anna Humphrey ; illustrated by Mike Deas.
Other titles: Bee and Flea, and the compost caper | Compost caper
Names: Humphrey, Anna, author. | Deas, Mike, 1982- illustrator.
Identifiers: Canadiana (print) 20210219181 | Canadiana (ebook) 20210219211
ISBN 9781771474207 (hardcover) | ISBN 9781771475297 (EPUB)
ISBN 9781771475303 (Kindle)
Classification: LCC PS8615.U457 B44 2022 | DDC jC813/.6—dc23

Edited by Sarah Howden | Designed by Alisa Baldwin

Manufactured in Guangdong Province, Dongguan City, China, in September 2021, by Toppan Leefung Packaging & Printing (Dongguan) Co., Ltd. | Job #BAYDC101

A   B   C   D   E   F

ONTARIO ARTS COUNCIL
CONSEIL DES ARTS DE L'ONTARIO
an Ontario government agency
un organisme du gouvernement de l'Ontario

Canada Council
for the Arts
Conseil des Arts
du Canada

Canada

MIX
Paper from
responsible sources
FSC® C104723

Publisher of Chirp, Chickadee and OWL
www.owlkidsbooks.com

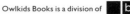 Owlkids Books is a division of  bayard canada

Bee & Flea
and the Compost Caper

WRITTEN BY
ANNA HUMPHREY

WITH ILLUSTRATIONS BY
MIKE DEAS

OWLKIDS BOOKS

Chapter 1

THE
F.L.E.A.

Bee lived in the big backyard. It was beautiful, with winding walkways and bountiful blossoms, but it was also boring—or so she thought.

"Daisies … done."

After three long days of hard work, Bee checked the pollinated flowers off her list with a small satisfied smile.

Then she glanced down at the next item.

"Dandelions?!"

Thousands of yellow blooms bobbed atop the vast green lawn.

"This is going to take FOREVER." Bee moaned and flopped down in the middle of her last daisy. "I can't face it," she said, even though she knew she'd eventually get up and put one mandible in front of the other. After all, it's what bees were born to do.

But before she could take her next weary breath—

"WRONG WAY!"

The daisy stem trembled.

Something was galumphing through the flowers toward her.

"STOP THIS SECOND!"

The gardener's wheezy old wiener dog emerged from a patch of petunias.

"IN THE NAME OF THE LAW ..."

Bee sat up, shook off some pollen dust, and looked around, puzzled. Who was talking? The shrill, shouty voice didn't match the squat, sullen dog. What's more, his mouth wasn't moving.

"TURN. AROUND. NOW."

"Who, me?" Bee fluttered her wings in panic.

"Not *you*! The dog!" the voice yelled. "But you might want to move, too, because any second now—"

Bee buzzed onto a different daisy just as the dog lifted his leg.

"Ha! Told ya!" the voice said, then it went back

to shouting. "STOP IT! YOU CAN PEE ON YOUR BREAK." This was followed by a grumble. "For the love of peat moss, I've met mealworm larvae less deaf than you, dog!"

Bee followed the sound. She stared extremely hard. And then she saw it: a flea standing on the dog's head. But not just any flea. A flea wearing purple horn-rimmed glasses and a matching purple fanny pack.

Bee watched as the small, loud flea burrowed beneath the flop of the dog's ear.

"THIS IS YOUR LAST WARNING!" she hollered.

"TURN. AROUND."

At last, the dog heard.

He spun twice on the spot. Then, with a high-pitched moan like the air going out of a balloon, he sank to the ground and fell asleep in the shade.

"Oh, you've *gotta* be kidding me!" The flea marched out from under the dog's ear and down the bridge of his nose. She threw her claws up in the air. "That's the third nap my driver's taken today! What's a professional parasite gotta do to get some decent help around here?"

"Hello? Um, hi there," Bee said. "Maybe I could help?"

"What?" Flea looked around frantically, as if she'd forgotten Bee was there. "Who said that?"

"It's me." Bee waved.

"Oh. You?" Flea narrowed her eyes. "How could you help?" She scratched her head. "Are you familiar with the policies and procedures of the F.L.E.A.?"

"The F.L.E.A.?"

"The Fenced-in-area Law Enforcement Agency." Flea waved four of her six legs wildly. "Who do you think serves, protects, and upholds the laws of nature in this fenced-in area?"

"I guess I never really thought about it," Bee admitted.

Beetles burrowed, ants paraded, but nothing illegal ever happened in the yard. In fact, aside from Bee's thousands of hive sisters buzzily working away, barely *anything* happened at all.

"The F.L.E.A. never rests." Flea puffed out her chest and marched back and forth across the dog's nose. "Rain or shine. Fair or frosty. Foggy or"—she stopped and furrowed her brow—"not foggy. Whenever there's trouble, F.L.E.A.'s there on the double."

"According to that, shouldn't it be on the *single*?" Bee pointed at a shiny gold star that Flea had pinned to her fanny pack. It might have been

a picky detail, but Bee was a bit of a stickler for correctness.

"On the single, on the double, on the sixty-three divided by two hundred and eleventeen— what matters is that the F.L.E.A. upholds the letter of the law. Which is *L*," Flea added, "for law enforcement."

Bee leaned forward. "So that means you solve crimes?"

Flea gave a curt nod.

"Stop backyard bandits?"

"Of course!" Flea declared.

"Rid the yard of evil?"

"All in a day's work," Flea said with a grand sweep of her front legs.

"Well, that sounds exciting," Bee said.

And then it hit her like a hunk of honeycomb to the head. This was it! Her chance to leave behind the dreary dandelions and be part of something thrilling.

Bee pointed to the snoring dog, whose cheek now rested in a puddle of drool. "Didn't you *just* say you could use a new driver?"

"You? My driver?" Flea seemed to consider it for a split second, then chuckled softly. "I don't mean to laugh, but do you even have a driver's license?"

"Oh." Bee frowned. "No."

Well, that was that. Back to the dandelions. Bee tightened the blade of grass she wore as a holster and had started to slip her clipboard into it when—

"Wait a second! What if I take notes for you?" She showed Flea her clipboard and beeswax crayon. "I could keep track of clues and things. I'm extremely organized. And an excellent speller."

Flea grimaced. "Hmmm … yeah. Nothing personal, Bee, but I've always worked alone. I mean, except for Thunder here, when he's not asleep." Flea pushed her glasses up her nose, then turned back to the snoozing dog with a heavy sigh.

Bee holstered her clipboard and sighed too. "Well, then, good luck on your exciting adventures, Flea." She couldn't keep the disappointment from her voice as she scanned the yard again. "I guess I'd better get busy, flying from dandelion to dandelion, to dandelion, to dandelion, to dandelion, to dandelion …"

Suddenly, Flea's antennae sprang up. She whirled on the spot. "Hold it right there, honeybee! Wait just one insecty-second! Did you just say you could *fly*?"

Chapter 2

A
DRIVER
WHO FLIES

With a surprisingly powerful leap, Flea sprung from the dog's nose onto Bee's back. She began examining Bee's wings, tugging them this way and that.

"Hey! Stop that!" Bee tried to swat her away.

"Why didn't you say you could fly?" Flea said as she let Bee's wings drop.

"Because …" Bee shrugged. "Well, because all bees can fly."

"Well, of course *all bees* can fly." Flea hopped off Bee's back and paced along the daisy stem. "That's common knowledge. Me, I'm more into *uncommon* knowledge. For example"—she pointed out a fly that had just landed in some fresh soil the gardener had put down earlier that morning—"did you know that houseflies upchuck on their food to soften it before they eat it?"

Bee hadn't known that, and now she desperately wished she could *un-know* it. Born and raised in a world of sweet honey, soft breezes, and fragrant flowers, she preferred to look away whenever she saw a spider mummifying a moth in its wicked web or maggots wriggling in the muck.

"That's … um …" Bee was searching for the right word to describe fly vomit without seeming rude. "Unpleasant," she said finally. And, oh, if

17

she'd had any inkling how much grosser things were about to get!

"Unpleasant?" Flea scoffed. "Not at all! Think of it like special sauce."

Bee couldn't help it. She gagged.

"Anyhoo," Flea went on cheerfully, "it's settled. Since you're a bee, and we all know bees can fly, you can be my driver who flies. On a trial basis, of course."

"Really?" Bee smiled. "Okay, then." She stretched her wings to warm them up. "You won't be sorry, Flea! I'll make an excellent driver who flies. But wait! Couldn't we just say 'flier'? Or 'pilot'?"

The odd little flea didn't seem interested in these suggestions. She was busy rummaging through her fanny pack, pulling out things like …

- a flea-sized detective's hat made of dried leaves

- a miniature corncob pipe

- a tube of poppy-red lipstick, which she applied generously before tossing aside

"Aha! There it is!"

Flea selected a tiny sprout just beginning to grow from a crack in a round seed.

"Is that a s—?" Bee was going to say "seed from a tomato plant," but Flea interrupted.

"Yuppers! A genuine F.L.E.A.-issued sundial. The time"—Flea consulted the tomato seed—"is approximately oh-nine-hundred hours." She licked the tip of one claw and held it up. "There's a southwesterly breeze. The temperature is hot, with a chance of getting way hotter, and"—she leaned to one side and cupped a claw around her ear as if listening to a far-off noise—"according to reports from the Cricket Communications Network, there's a disturbance at the compost heap. The F.L.E.A. needs its finest and only agent and her temporary

20

driver who flies. Are you up to the task, Bee?"

"Oh. The compost heap?"

Bee hadn't meant to hesitate, but her antennae—which she used to smell—were extra sensitive. They helped her make out the merest whisper of a wisteria blossom floating on the breeze. So that giant pile of rotting food the gardener kept in the corner of the yard? Well, just the *thought* of the stink was enough to make Bee want to bury her face in a begonia.

"Yuppity doodle! The compost heap!" Flea cried. "A hot spot of rot. Well, usually. But today, something sinister is afoot."

"Something sinister?" Bee repeated. "That's intriguing." Maybe the smell wouldn't be *that* bad? "All right," she said, making up her mind.

"Let's do it. To the compost heap!"

Flea shrugged. "We don't have to be *that* hasty. You can't uphold the law on an empty stomach, am I right? Before we go, a quick snackity snack."

Flea dug through her fanny pack, and Bee watched in fascination again as things sailed past:

- a telescope made from a hollow stem

- a safety vest of orange and yellow flower petals

- a small kazoo carved from a stick

Then: "Ta-da! My twirly straw!"

Flea boinged back onto Thunder, bit him just above the ear, plunged her straw into the hole, and drank deeply, making a glug-glug noise with each swallow.

"Y-you aren't—?" Bee clapped a hand over

her mouth. "Are you actually drinking—?" She felt woozy.

"Dog's blood?" Flea wiped the back of her claw across her face. "Only when I can't find a nice juicy cat." She took another big swallow just before Thunder stirred in his sleep and scratched at his ear. She only just managed to leap out of the way in time.

Boing. Boing.

Another two leaps and she landed squarely on Bee's thorax. "Okeydokey," she announced. "All set!" She grabbed hold of Bee's antennae and began to whirl them in circles, making a dreadful wailing noise: "WEEE-OOOOO! WEEE-OOOOO! WEEE-OOOOO!"

Bee looked up at Flea.

"Driver who flies! What's the holdup?" Flea asked, then she began to spin and wail again. "WEEE-OOOOO! WEEE-OOOOO!"

Bee wasn't sure if she'd ever met an odder or more irritating creature in all her life. The lack of basic manners, the gross facts, the blood glugging ...

"I thought it was common knowledge," Flea whispered out the side of her mouth, "but the sirens mean you're supposed to rush to the emergency, Bee."

Then again, an *emergency*. It really *was* exciting.

I'll fly the flea, she said to herself. But just this once. If I don't like it, I can always go back to the dreary dandelions.

"Giddyup!" Flea cried, bouncing her heels against Bee's sides.

Bee gritted her mouthparts.

Just this once, she told herself again.

With sirens blaring, she took off across the yard.

Chapter 3

THE MAGIC GLASSES

The compost bin wasn't far by air. They arrived within seconds.

"Bring us in for a landing on that head of lettuce, Bee," Flea instructed.

"You know, it wouldn't hurt you to say 'please,'" Bee pointed out, but she veered sharply to the left anyway, aiming for the wilted greens.

She was all set to make a flawless landing when—

"Whoooooooah!" Bee's feet skidded across the slick surface. Then: "Oof!" She slid right over the lettuce and crashed headfirst into a pile of slime-covered scallions.

Bee crawled out of the onion pile with a foreleg clapped over her mouth. Green ooze dripped from her antennae and coated her wings. "Oh! So awful!" she cried.

"Too true, Bee." Flea scurried out and casually shook green gloop off one leg. "I wasn't going to say it, but that was awful. When you said you could fly, I figured you could land too. You'll wanna work on that."

Before Bee could point out that Flea was the one who'd picked the liquidy landing spot, the smaller insect went marching off.

"ATTENTION! This is the F.L.E.A. speaking," she

yelled. "Stop making that racket right this second."

Bee looked left.

Bee looked right.

A few flies buzzed overhead, landing every

so often (probably to vomit on things before

they ate them, Bee thought with a shudder), but

except for their *buzz-buzz* and Flea's shouting,

Bee couldn't hear any racket.

"Cease your shenanigans!" Flea scolded the withered lettuce.

Somewhere up in a tree, a bird chirped softly.

An earthworm inched along, stopped, yawned, and inched onward.

"You know," Bee began gently, because someone had to say something, "it's slick and slimy, but that lettuce isn't making any noise."

Flea rolled her eyes. "Well, of course it isn't! It's way past its crispy-crunchy days. I was talking to the billions and billions of unruly rascals." She flailed her front legs around at the wilted veggies. "STOPPPP SHOUTING!" Flea shouted so loudly that Bee had to cover her ears.

Bee watched as a hard-backed beetle scurried

silently under a leaf and a parade of tiny ants carried food scraps from here to there without so much as a peep.

"I just remembered," Bee said, backing away, "I never did get my flyer's license either." She could see there was no use arguing. "It's a shame, but I guess I can't work for the F.L.E.A. after all."

Flea, who was still marching back and forth in front of the lettuce, didn't seem to hear Bee. "I demand order in this decay!" she said.

"Plus, I've already got a full-time job," Bee explained. "A yard full of flowers isn't going to pollinate itself." She chuckled, then flew up onto the handle of a shovel that was leaning against the compost bin. "Nice meeting you, Flea. But off I go!"

Suddenly, Flea spun around and planted her claws on the sides of her abdomen. "Wait a second." She frowned. "Wait *just a second*. Bees don't need a license to fly!"

"I ... um, well ..." Bee crossed her mandibles sheepishly.

"You're trying to buzz off work early." Flea pointed an accusing claw.

"What?! No!" Bee answered, all in a flap. "I just think it might be best for me to get back to my flowers. Because you might be"—how could she put it nicely?—"imagining things," she finished. "For example, since we arrived, you've been shouting nonstop at nobody at all."

"Well, well, well!" Flea appeared to address the lettuce again. "Did you hear that, Mr. Potworm? She just called you—and all your friends and family—*nobody at all*."

Bee followed Flea's gaze.

"You've insulted dear old Mr. Potworm, Bee," Flea said. "He's very hurt by your words. Can't you see that?"

Bee could not.

"I've never seen him like this." Flea shook her head sadly. "He's always smiling and joking. Just the other day, he said to me, 'Flea, did you hear about the amoeba that called a restaurant to make a reservation?'" Flea pattered out a drumroll against her femurs. "He said, 'Table for one, please. It's just *amoeba* myself.'"

Flea dissolved into gales of laughter, clutching at her sides while Bee looked on with growing concern.

"Get it?" Flea gasped for breath. "Amoeba? A-me-by myself?"

Bee didn't get it.

"Oh, Mr. Potworm"—Flea wiped a tear from her eye—"you kill me. Don't you let this silly bee upset you. You're not *nobody at all*." She gave Bee a disapproving look. "I mean, really, Bee? How RUDE!"

"Now, wait just a second!" Bee flew back down onto the heap. If there was one thing she couldn't stand, it was someone doubting her manners— least of all a shouting, blood-glugging flea. "You're calling *me* rude? That's quite enough." She shook the last drop of onion goo off her wings and spread them wide. "Goodbye forever."

"No!" Flea shouted. "Don't go." Her voice softened. "Not yet." She smacked herself in the forehead. "I see the problem now! I get why you're having such a hard time focusing on your F.L.E.A. duties."

Because there is no F.L.E.A., Bee thought. Because the entire thing is a load of hooey.

"It's because you're not wearing your official uniform!" Flea said. "Just wait! You'll see." Flea unzipped her purple fanny pack and once again began pulling things out and tossing them aside:

- a length of rope made of braided grass

- a pair of twiggy handcuffs with a maple key

- an oversized beach umbrella made of a Chinese lantern pod

"Aha!"

Flea unfolded a bright purple fanny pack identical to her own, only larger and without a gold star badge. She bounded onto Bee's back and began to stretch the straps around her big furry belly.

"Hmmm," Flea remarked as she worked, "mixing polka dots and stripes—so fashion-forward."

"What are you—?" Bee looked over her shoulder. "Stop that!"

"But you've got to wear a tool tote, Bee," Flea said matter-of-factly. "Where else are you going to store your magical glasses?"

"My what?"

"Suck in, Bee! Just. One. Last. Tug."

The clasp connected with a snap that left Bee gasping for breath.

There was a *zip-zip* as Flea opened the new fanny pack. "Here you go." She reached around Bee's head. "These should fit."

"Flea!" Bee snapped. "I refuse to wear a pair of silly horn-rimmed glass—"

But then Bee stopped cold.

She staggered backward.

"Holy honey!" she said.

Because—where before there'd been only brown banana peels, mold-ridden melon rinds, and that slimy head of lettuce—an entire universe of the teeniest-tiniest proportions had come into focus.

Chapter 4

THE
LITTLEST
LAWBREAKERS

The compost heap was bursting with life! There were the small ants Bee had noticed earlier. And worms. Loads of worms. Red wigglers and nightcrawlers and much tinier ones too. Even— yes!—one especially itty-bitty worm, right near the lettuce. He was nearly transparent and wore a bow tie made from a nibbled-up bit of orange peel.

"Is that dear old Mr. Potworm?" Bee asked.

"The one and the only," Flea answered.

"I can't really believe … wow!" Bee tried to take it all in. "I'm sorry, sir," she called out to the tiny worm. "I shouldn't have called you nobody. It's just that clearly I didn't see you there before."

Mr. Potworm scowled. His mouth moved, but no sound came out. At least, no sound Bee could hear.

Flea cringed. "Bee. Oh, Bee. Now you've *really* upset him."

"I did? How?"

"*Clearly* you didn't see him there?" Flea shook her head. "Talk about an insulting thing to say to a see-through worm."

Bee gasped. "That's not what I meant. Mr. Potworm—" But before she could apologize again, the little worm went wriggling away. And anyway, she was soon distracted by the rest of the scene that had come into focus through her official F.L.E.A.-issued glasses.

Tiny transparent worms were just the start.

There were quick skittery brown creatures that looked like baby spiders, reddish ones with pincers waving wildly, and—even tinier than all of those— clear hairy blobs with tails that jiggled like bits of royal jelly. Above all that, along with the houseflies, flew many tiny aerial insects normally too teensy to be noticed.

But these creatures weren't just peacefully crawling and flying around, enjoying the beautiful morning. Oh no! *Not at all.*

"Break it up. Break it up, you two," Flea told a pincered critter and an eight-legged bug that were wrestling in the muck.

"Rethink that risky behavior," she hollered at a reddish one that was sliding down a slimy cucumber peel using a bit of eggshell as a surfboard.

"That's it. Enough! I'm writing you all tickets." Flea pulled a booklet out of her tool tote and began to scribble in it. "Reckless running. Disruptive digging. Messing up the mud." She threw little scraps of paper toward various creatures as they ran amok around her.

It was complete and total chaos.

"Oh no!" Bee covered her eyes. "I think that one just ate its friend!"

Flea followed Bee's horrified gaze. Eight legs were indeed sticking out of the pincer bug's mouth.

"SPIT HIM OUT!" Flea ordered.

But the bug just grinned and swallowed.

"You see, Bee?" Flea shook her head. "You see what the F.L.E.A. deals with, day in and day out?"

Bee *did* see. In fact, her eyes had never been wider.

Maybe coming here had been a rotten idea after all.

"All right," Flea told the full-tummied pincer bug. "I'm letting you off easy. But next time I catch you eating your buddy, you're in BIG TROUBLE. Understand?"

Flea tucked her ticket book away and motioned to the still-stunned Bee. "Come on. Let's go find someone to help us get to the bottom of this. I know just the critter."

Chapter 5

A
LOTTA
ROTTA

They marched over hills of browning broccoli, across plains of potato peels, through ponds of putrid pineapple juice.

All the while, Flea hollered orders and handed out tickets.

And all the while, Bee's mind boggled at the sights she saw.

"That's your last warning, woodlice!" Flea told a group of armor-plated bugs that were curling into balls and rolling through a pile of damp leaves.

Meanwhile, others ran in wild circles and

whacked each other on the head with slivers

they'd peeled off an old twig.

As Flea marched ahead, Bee took out her

clipboard and wrote a few quick notes:

Observations
- Critter Chaos
- Bug Battles

"Nematodes! Stop bullying the bacteria!" Flea said.

She seemed to be talking to a pack of little worms that were nudging something soft and fuzzy that clung to a strawberry.

Bee got a little closer and peered through her glasses. The fuzz was made up of tiny threads. Millions of them. They were swaying back and forth, bonking into each other like unruly guests at a party.

"Those fuzzy things! They're alive?" she gasped.

"Of course," Flea answered. "How else could they dance such a graceful bacteria ballet?"

Flea did a few pirouettes and hummed a tune as she pranced on.

Bee watched in horror as a little worm stuffed its

48

cheeks full of wriggling bacteria. Then she added

to her notes:

- Bungled Ballet
- Greedy Gobbling

Bop! Something hit the back of Bee's head. She turned and eyed a crowd of eight-legged critters that seemed to be playing a fast-paced game with a lot of throwing, dodging, and ducking.

"Was that a … snowball?" Bee asked, then felt silly. After all, it was summer. There wasn't any snow. What's more, the balls the critters were throwing weren't white but brown.

Bee's antennae wilted as she realized—

"Are they throwing …?" She covered her eyes with her mandibles. "POOP?!"

Flea seemed unbothered. "You betcha. Mites are all about poop," she said. "They make it, carry it, play with it. Whoa, Bee! Duck!" she yelled, pulling Bee down just in time to avoid being hit in the head with a second foul ball.

"There's nothing like a good game of dodge-poop on a sunny day, but you've gotta keep your wits about you," Flea said as they cowered. "The brown mites are especially quick. See how they're ganging up on the red and white teams? They've even been known to eat their opponents when things don't go their way."

"That's horrifying!" Bee said.

"Nah!" Flea waved a claw dismissively. "The Arachnids are just a super-competitive family."

"Wait! They're *family*? That's even worse!"

"Is it?" Flea gave Bee a doubtful glance. "Are you telling me you've never felt like biting your sisters' heads off?"

"What?!" Bee said. "Of course not!"

"Sure, sure." Flea winked. "Aha! There's Rodney

the Rotifer's place up ahead. He'll explain this mess."

Flea marched on and Bee followed behind.

- Pooping
- Pooping
- Feasting on Family
- Plenty More Pooping

Chapter 6

RODNEY'S BREAKFAST

They soon arrived at the gooey brown banana peel.

"Rodney the Rotifer!" Flea cried. "Long time no see."

Even with her magic glasses, Bee had to squint to find Rodney. The rotifer was a clear worm like Mr. Potworm, but smaller, blobbier—and without the bow tie.

"I'm here for an official statement," Flea told

Rodney, who was floating in a thin slime of ooze that clung to the peel. "We'd like to know how this all began."

"Right," Bee chimed in. "Like why are the bugs eating each other and pooping everywhere and just going BANANAS?"

Flea winced.

"What? What'd I say now?"

"Going *bananas*," Flea repeated in a whisper. She motioned toward the peel where Rodney lived. "Plus, Rodney here eats his friends all the time. And everybody poops, Bee." Flea rolled her eyes. "Look, why don't you just leave the talking to me?"

Bee felt like she'd been walloped by a wet leaf.

"Hang on a sec there, Rodney." Flea unzipped her tool tote and started to dig through. Out came:

- a megaphone made from a snowdrop blossom

- some birchbark binoculars

- a fluffy duster made of hummingbird feathers

"Aha!" Flea pulled out a blueberry with

buttons on it, followed by a pair of poppy-seed headphones and a tiny pine-cone microphone. "State-of-the-art Bluefruit audio recording equipment," she explained as she fiddled with the buttons on the blueberry. "Don't want to miss a detail. Only …" She tilted the blueberry this way and that. "Hmmm, must be out of juice."

"That's all right!" Bee said, seeing her chance to make up for the banana blunder. She whipped out her clipboard and stood at the ready. "I'll take notes for you. Remember? I'm a great speller."

"Well …" Flea hesitated a moment. "I guess we can try that." She put down the blueberry. "Start by writing Rodney's name."

Bee lined up the letters in a tidy row.

R-O-D-N-E-Y

"Not bad," Flea said after checking the work carefully.

Bee couldn't help but smile. Finally, her chance to shine!

"Now put down his last name. Rodney's part of the Pseudocoelomate family."

Bee's mouth dropped open. "Soodo-what?"

"Now *there's* a family that goes above and beyond when it comes to eating each other, eh, Rodney? Remember the time your great-granny, Tootsie, mistook her own toes for bits of bacteria and gobbled them up?"

Flea erupted into laughter while Bee stood by, worrying over the hard word.

"They called her Tootsie Toeless from then on." Flea wiped a tear from her eye. "Anyhoo," she said,

turning to Bee, "let's get on with it."

Bee looked at her clipboard. The only thing to do was to sound it out. "Soo-doe-SEE-lo-mate," she muttered.

S-U-D

Flea tapped a back leg impatiently.

"BEE!" Flea took the clipboard with a frown. "Don't you know pseudocoelomate starts with a silent *P*?"

Bee gaped as Flea took her crayon to correct the spelling. Whoever heard of a silent *P*?

"Never mind." Flea picked up her blueberry and whacked it hard with the back of her claw. The buttons lit up. "There! See? Problem solved."

But Bee, who was left with nothing to do, wasn't so sure.

"Now, Rodney"—Flea held out the microphone—"in your own words, tell me what started all this havoc and hoopla."

But as was the case with Mr. Potworm, Bee couldn't make out Rodney's words.

"It all began this morning," Flea reported.

Bee leaned forward, waiting to learn about the thrilling events that had kicked off the kerfuffle.

"Rodney woke up to a deafening racket," Flea narrated.

If Bee had been sitting, she'd have been on the edge of her seat.

"There was a frightening avalanche. Food was flying!"

"An avalanche? How dangerous!" Bee said, her eyes wide

"And then …" Flea paused, building the suspense. "And then …" She paused again. "He had breakfast."

"Breakfast?" Bee blinked.

"He started with a side of dead bacteria." Flea

listened some more. "And a strong, hot cup of slime." She nodded for Rodney to go on.

Flea listened for a long time, muttering to Bee about how, exactly, the cup of slime had been brewed and its various flavor notes. Finally, just when Bee wasn't sure she could take another minute—

"Aha!" Flea exclaimed.

Bee perked up. Here it came. Something huge about all the hullabaloo!

"And then an amuse-bouche of algae," Flea said.

Bee groaned.

"That means a fancy little snack. I can spell it for you, if you'd like. Uh-huh. And then a tasty bite of—"

"Flea!" Bee interrupted.

"What?"

"Well …" Bee didn't want to hurt Rodney's feelings again, but if listening to the details of someone else's breakfast was really what the F.L.E.A. was all about, it wasn't that much more fun than a lawn full of dandelions. "Well …" Bee began again. "Couldn't Rodney focus on the more *interesting* parts of the story. You know—more about the avalanche and the racket? Less about … breakfast?"

"What could be more interesting than breakfast?" Flea asked in disbelief.

"I don't know. Maybe something else. Something more … *exciting*?"

"Huh." Flea scratched her head. "You want excitement, eh?"

"I do!" Bee said. "I really do."

Flea paused dramatically. "You want fascinating and interesting?"

"Oh yes," Bee said. "Please!"

"Then open up your tool tote, Bee. Because oh boy, have I got a job for you!"

Chapter 7

GARBAGE DUTY

Bee reached for the zipper of her fanny pack, her mind racing. What incredible gear would she find inside?

A magical parachute made of petunia petals?

A sword forged from a thistle spike?

A high-powered speedboat that was once an empty peanut shell?

Bee's hand closed around something crinkly and slippery. She pulled it out with trembling forelegs.

"Is it a cape?"

Flea grinned and clapped her claws. "It's way better than a cape, Bee." She grabbed the crinkly thing, shook it open, and presented it back to Bee with a flourish. "It's a garbage bag!"

"A *garbage* bag?"

"And that's not all! Reach in again."

Bee did, hoping for something much better. This time she felt a long, smooth object that was—"Ouch!"—sharp at one end.

"*And* a super-pointy garbage picky-uppy stick," Flea announced as Bee pulled out a whittled twig. "Congratulations, Bee! Now you can do something exciting." Flea was positively beaming.

"I—what?"

"Yes," Flea insisted. "You get to be the trash collector!"

"But that's not—"

"Sometimes things get tossed into the compost that don't belong," Flea went on, oblivious to Bee's distress. "You know—little stickers on fruit and vegetable peels, bits of plastic wrap, other noncompostables. You just never know quite what you'll find next. And *you*, my friend, get to save the day! Wow-ee zow-ee, are you ever lucky."

"Lucky?!"

"Enjoy the adventure!" Flea said, then clapped her earphones back on.

"But—" Bee began. "Are you serious? It's just that … I mean …"

Flea didn't hear a word of Bee's protest. "Uh-huh," she was saying. "Well, leaf particles *do* make a nice light brunch." She turned, smiled at Bee, and waved her off. "Although"—Flea looked back to Rodney—"personally I prefer a thick and creamy blood smoothie." She smacked her mouthparts.

"AAARGH!" Bee stomped off. "Trash collector?!"

She climbed a hill of beans and marched over an apple core. "How dull!" She stabbed a sticker on a peach peel with her twig and put it into her bag. "I might as well be pollinating an acre of asparagus."

She trudged back through the group of mites. They seemed to be taking a break from their wild game of dodge-poop. Now they were fighting over a bunch of moldy grapes. It made Bee's stomach turn.

"Move it!" she said, pushing through them to get to a little piece of cellophane. "Important, exciting work to do, you know. Serving the F.L.E.A." She brought her pointy stick down but missed the plastic wrap entirely, stabbing a grape instead. Oozy liquid shot out and sprayed all over her glasses.

"Ugh!" She wiped at the lenses with her
mandibles. "What are *you* looking at?" she
snapped at the worms on the strawberry. They'd
stopped feasting on fuzz long enough to look up
and stare. "Haven't you ever seen someone hard

at work before? No, I guess you haven't. Because all you do is eat. And poop."

Bee raised her pointy picker-upper and was about to bring it down hard on a piece of waxed paper when a little head with an orange-peel bow tie popped out from underneath.

"Oh, it's you!" Bee said, not as kindly as she could have.

Mr. Potworm grimaced.

"Well, you don't have to look at me like *that*." Bee lowered her stick. "I wouldn't have stabbed you. I just didn't see you. And no, it's not because you're transparent," she added. "But you've got to admit, that doesn't help."

At that, Mr. Potworm shook his head and crawled off toward the strawberry.

"And a pleasant day to you too," Bee called after him.

Mr. Potworm stopped, turned to glare at her, and—worst of all—began to wriggle his rear end in the air.

"Stop that this second!" Bee said.

And then, as if the bum wriggling wasn't ill-mannered enough—well, there's no way to put it delicately: Mr. Potworm started to poop, right there in front of her!

"Enough!" Bee couldn't take it a moment longer. She threw down her pointy stick and garbage bag. Then she yelled, louder than she'd ever yelled anything in her entire life: "ENOOOOOOOOUGH!"

Mr. Potworm's mouth opened in an O. The mites called a time-out from their grape munching to

gawk. Even the bacteria stopped dancing and turned to stare.

"I quit! You hear me? I QUIT! Pollinating flowers may be boring, but at least it's useful. I mean, really! Running around willy-nilly? Eating your family? Stuffing your faces and pooping all over?"

Bee backed away, shaking her head.

"All of you"—she pointed to the mites, the worms, the bacteria—"and Flea most of all, you're … well, there's just no other word for it: DISGUS—"

But at that moment, Bee took another big step backward and—

"Wha-wha-whoooah!" She staggered, slipped, and fell right into a wormhole.

Chapter 8

THE DEEP, DARK HOLE

The hole was deep. The hole was dark. The hole was dirty. And the hole was …

"Disgusting!" Bee repeated quietly—but only after her wildly beating heart had settled and she'd started to realize the trouble she was in.

For many long minutes, she'd wriggled and jiggled and tried to work her way free, but it was no use. The hole was narrow, and the purple fanny pack Flea had clipped around her abdomen was

so big that she was firmly wedged in. Next, she'd

tried calling for help, yelling out Flea's name at

the top of her lungs. But she couldn't yell as loud

as Flea could. And after all, Flea was back at the

banana peel, wearing her poppy-seed headphones.

There was no way she'd hear Bee's cries.

Things seemed completely hopeless until—

"Oh, hello!" Bee caught sight of a pair of eight-legged red critters that had just crawled down beside her. "I'm Bee. We met before. Up there."

The creatures climbed atop her head and sat for a moment.

"And you are …?" She searched her memory. "Mites! From the Arachnid family."

They nodded.

She looked up at them pleadingly. "I wonder if I could ask you an itty-bitty favor. Not that you're itty-bitty," she added quickly. "That's not what I meant. You're just the exact perfect size for mites."

They didn't seem offended, so she carried on. "See, I've fallen into this deep, dark hole and

I can't get out. If you could just go and tell my friend Flea ..."

The first mite said something to the second. They argued back and forth for a moment and then, all at once, pooped. Right on Bee's head! They laughed hysterically.

"Really?!" Bee said as they scurried down her thorax and burrowed deeper into the hole. "That's how you help someone in need?" She

sighed. "I guess I did just call them disgusting."

She tilted her head this way and that, and finally the poop rolled off—only to topple down into her holster.

"Great!" she muttered.

Bee pulled out the clipboard and tried to brush the poop off her notes. It left a smudge.

Observations
- Critter Chaos
- Bug Battles
- Bungled Ballet
- Greedy Gobbling
- Pooping
- Pooping
- Feasting on Family
- Plenty More Pooping

"Well," she said as she reread the list, "I guess I shouldn't be surprised they pooped on my head. They poop everywhere else. Eat and poop. Eat and poop. It's all they do around here. It's so gross and stinky and—wait a second." Bee held the stained clipboard up to her antennae.

It wasn't *stinky* at all!

Instead, the smell was familiar. It reminded her of flowers, but not the sweet perfume of blossoms. It was rich, fragrant, and earthy. Like …

"Soil!" Bee said in wonder. "Soil!" she said again. Because quite suddenly, the pieces of a great (but tiny) puzzle had clicked together in her mind.

"FLEAAAAAAAA!" she cried as loud as she could. "FLEEEAAAAAAA!"

Bee had just solved the mystery, and she

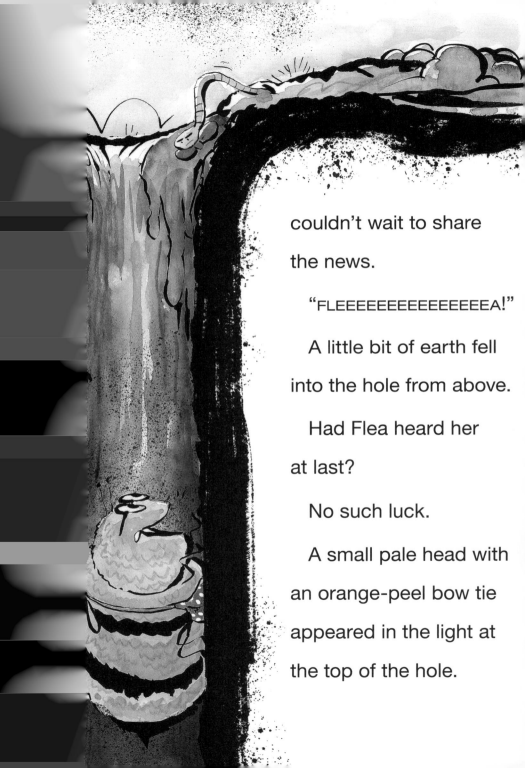

couldn't wait to share
the news.

"FLEEEEEEEEEEEEEEEA!"

A little bit of earth fell
into the hole from above.

Had Flea heard her
at last?

No such luck.

A small pale head with
an orange-peel bow tie
appeared in the light at
the top of the hole.

"Mr. Potworm!" said Bee, nearly in tears. "Am I ever glad to see you!"

She could tell from the frown on his face that Mr. Potworm didn't feel the same. He turned to go.

"No, wait! Please."

Mr. Potworm paused and gave her a doubtful look.

"I was wrong. So wrong. I see you *plainly* now," Bee said, choosing her words carefully. "I recognize the important work you poo—I mean, *do*. And … well, I owe you—and everyone else— a *huge* apology."

Chapter 9

A
PEST

Dear old Mr. Potworm must have slithered to Rodney the Rotifer's banana peel as quickly as he could, because it wasn't long before Bee heard Flea's voice coming from up above.

"Bee? What are you doing *now*? This is no time for exploring holes."

"Flea!" said Bee with great relief. "I'm not exploring. I'm stuck!"

"What's that? CAN'T HEAR YOU," yelled

Flea—who, Bee noticed, was still wearing her headphones. "Hang on a sec. I'm coming down."

"No, Flea! Don't!" Bee said.

But it was too late. Flea had already flung herself into the hole and landed on top of Bee's head, right between her antennae.

"That's better," Flea said, taking off the headphones. "You were saying?"

"I was saying, I've fallen into this deep, dark hole."

"Ha!" Flea said. "What a coinkydink. Me too!"

Bee groaned.

"It's also lousy timing," Flea said. "Rodney was just about done with brunch. After lunch and dinner, I'll bet you anything he was going to fill me in on how the chaos got rolling. But now we'll never ever know."

Bee buzzed with excitement despite their predicament. "Actually, Flea, I think I've figured out what's going on. It's not chaos! This compost heap is doing exactly what it needs to do to help the garden."

Flea shook her head. "But I've given out fifty-five tickets already. No, wait—fifty-six. I stopped a woodlouse on my way over here and wrote her up for barbaric bark crunching."

"But you didn't need to," Bee said, "because there's a perfectly good reason for what's going on. Earlier, the gardener spread soil on the flower beds. Rich, fragrant soil. Just like this soil here."

Bee pinched off a bit of the earth and held it up for Flea to see.

"He must have stirred up the compost and scooped some out. *That* was the disturbance reported by the Cricket Communications Network. It's why the creatures are all worked up. But look!" She showed Flea her clipboard. "Greedy gobbling, feasting on family, plenty of pooping—it's not breaking the law at all! It's their life's work!"

Flea frowned and scratched her head.

"The critters eat the gardener's rotten veggies—
and each other," Bee continued, "and turn them
into soil by digesting them. So you see, everything
is as it should be! The F.L.E.A. isn't needed here."

"Not … needed?" Flea's face fell, but Bee was
too busy explaining her Big Idea to notice.

"And I'm a part of it too." Bee wiggled her
antennae excitedly. She grabbed her beeswax
crayon, flipped to a fresh page on her clipboard,
and started to draw. "Flowers grow in soil," she
said, sketching a blossom. "I pollinate them." She
added an arrow to a bee. "Fruits and veggies
sprout, and the gardener eats them," she said,
drawing a ripe apple, then a stick figure. "He

88

puts the peels and cores in the compost, which

the littlest critters make back into soil." Now she

drew Mr. Potworm and his bow tie. "And that gets

spread in the garden, for the whole thing to start

again!" She drew an arrow back to the flower.

"We're all part of the same spectacular cycle! I

can't believe it, Flea. I've never been so excited to

pollinate dandelions. In fact, I can hardly wait! If we ever get out of this hole—"

Flea, who'd been pacing back and forth across Bee's head, stopped and let out a sudden wail. "Bee! This is TERRIBLE!"

Bee felt a tiny wet drop. "Flea? Are you … crying?" she asked.

"Of course I am!" Flea answered. "You'd cry, too, if you were good for nothing."

"What on earth are you talking about?" Bee asked.

"'Flea, your help isn't needed here. Flea, everyone's part of the super-duper cycle except you. Flea, you make me so, so itchy. Why don't you just go away?'" She sobbed huge salty tears. "I've heard it all before."

"But I thought … I mean, you're F.L.E.A. Agent 1 (and only 1). You work alone, remember?"

"Not because I want to. Because I *have* to! I'M A PEST!" Flea wailed. "A PARASITE! Nobody needs me. And nobody wants to spend time with me. They never have. And they never will."

And with that, Flea collapsed into a small heap and cried her tiny heart out.

Chapter 10

ONE
LARGE LEAP

At first, Bee didn't know what to do.

"There, there." She patted Flea gently on the back with one of her antennae.

Flea kept crying.

And crying.

Tear after tear ran down her face and dripped onto Bee's head.

"It's all right," Bee said as calmly as possible,

even though the wetter she got, the muckier the hole became.

"It's *not* all right!" Flea wailed. "I'm annoying! Irritating! Good for nothing but making dogs itchy!"

"That's not true," Bee said. "You're good for lots of things. I mean, without you, who would …?" She came up short. "I mean, who else could ever …?"

Flea gave a great snotty sniff.

"You make cats itchy, too, don't you?" Bee tried. "I bet you could make any animal at all itchy. That's not nothing."

"Oh, Bee," Flea said. "You're trying to cheer me up, but it won't work. I'm done. FINISHED. We may as well be stuck here forever."

Bee wasn't so sure.

Just then, Mr. Potworm appeared. Bee watched

as he stopped and said something to Flea.

"Not now. I'm in no mood for jokes," Flea
answered.

But Mr. Potworm continued to speak. She
listened, shrugged, listened some more—then
burst out laughing.

"What?" Bee asked.

Flea grinned through her tears. "How do fleas travel?" she asked.

Bee waited.

"They itch-hike!" Flea laughed again, then she caught her breath and spoke sternly. "All right, Mr. Potworm, move it along. Can't you see I'm busy wallowing in a pit of despair?"

Mr. Potworm adjusted his bow tie and tunneled on.

"Good joke, though," Bee called after him. "*Itch*-hike. I'm telling that to the girls if I ever get back to the hive. They'll never believe I heard it from a potworm. And all thanks to you, Flea."

Bee stopped.

"Wait a second!" she gasped. "That's it! *You* heard the joke! Because you can *hear* them.

Mr. Potworm, the mites, Rodney the Rotifer, the pincer bugs, the itty-bitty clear worms, and all the rest of the little creatures. You're the only one who can hear them!"

"Yeah, and a lot of good it does me," said Flea as a few more tears dripped off her face.

"A lot of good it does the REST OF US. Don't you see, Flea? Without you and your magic glasses and your purple fanny pack, I would never have known these creatures were here at all. You showed me!"

Flea sniffed. "I *showed* you?"

"You did! Because of you, I learned that—big, small, or teeny-tiny—we all depend on one another. And for the record, Flea," she added, hoping to stop the tears for good, "*I* like you."

"You do?" Flea asked.

"Of course I do!"

"Why?"

"Well …" Bee began. "You're enthusiastic."

"That's true!" Flea nodded. "I'm VERY enthusiastic! What else is great about me?"

"Well …" Bee didn't have a second idea lined up just yet. She had to think fast. "You're a wonderful yeller. You yell louder than anyone I've ever met. I can't come close to yelling as loud as you do. Trust me, I tried."

"I AM A SPECTACULAR YELLER," Flea yelled. "I'm pretty much THE YELLINGEST, right?"

The sound bounced off the walls of the hole, making Bee's entire body vibrate.

"What else?" Flea prompted.

Thankfully, Bee was on a roll. "Well, when you're not busy writing tickets, you listen to all the critters and laugh at their jokes and notice what they're good at, like throwing poop or eating family members. Plus, you came down here for me when I called." Bee realized something as she spoke the words. "When you set your mind to it, you're actually a pretty good friend, Flea."

"I am?" Flea seemed pleased for a moment, but then she frowned. "Only *pretty good*?"

"*Very* good," Bee said, stretching the truth. "Okay, *great*," she said when another tear fell.

"Don't you think," Flea said with a sniff, "if we're going to say 'great,' we might as well just go ahead and say 'best'?"

Bee sighed. "Sure, okay. Why not?"

"Woo-hoo," Flea yelled. "BEST! I'm the BEST

friend!"

And with that, she bounded up and out of the

hole in a single leap.

Chapter 11

A BIG PROMOTION

"Flea?!" Bee stared up. "This whole time you could have jumped out *that* easily?"

"Righty-ho! Fleas are excellent leapers," she called down.

"But"—Bee glared at her—"you said you were stuck in a pit of despair!"

"Oh, *that*? I was talking about the way I felt. It's called a metaphor, Bee. I can spell that for you if you'd like."

Flea unzipped her fanny pack and dug out a pulley system made of spiderwebs and twigs. She tossed one end into the hole and lassoed it around Bee's tummy in one smooth movement.

"Now you, on the other hand, are *literally* stuck," Flea said. She began to grunt and groan with the effort of reeling Bee up.

Bee gasped with relief as she surfaced from the wet, dark hole. She never thought she'd be so glad to see a pile of slimy vegetables—or to sit next to such an odd (and often irritating) little flea.

"So, best friend Bee ..." Flea did a little tap dance, waving her claws excitedly. "What best-friend thing do you wanna do first?"

Bee blinked at her.

"Make friendship bracelets? Or ... oh! Get started on our top-secret handshake? We could practice finishing each other's sentences. Or—"

"Get back to work?" Bee suggested hopefully.

"See, Bee? We're doing it already! That's what I was going to say! Get back to work. Only ... hold it, honeybee." Flea frowned. "Wait just an insecty-second. You mean back to work for the F.L.E.A., right?"

Bee looked around at the rotting vegetables and the little critters settling back into the soil after their wild day.

"I don't know." She scratched her head.

Once she'd got to know them, the creepy-crawly little critters weren't nearly as gross as she'd first thought. Actually, they were kind of fascinating. But did she really want to stay on with the F.L.E.A. permanently? Flea got to have all the fun. Bee was only a driver. And trash collector.

"Obviously," said Flea, as if reading her mind, "being my bestie comes with a promotion."

"It does?" Bee was listening now.

"Oh, sure. A BIG one."

Nobody had ever offered Bee a promotion before.

Flea grinned. "Close your eyes. I've got a super-duper surprise for you."

"Really?" Bee could picture the shiny gold badge: F.L.E.A. Agent 2.

There was the *zip-zip* of a fanny pack, then she felt a jiggling around her middle. Was Flea pinning it on?

"Okay! Open!"

F.L.E.A.
OFFICIAL
DRIVER-WHO-
FLIES

"Really?" Bee crinkled her antennae. After all, she hadn't *only* flown Flea to the heap. She'd taken notes! She'd put together the clues! She'd solved the mystery!

"Oh, fine," Flea muttered. "Close your eyes again."

When Bee opened them this time, she sighed.

If Flea noticed her friend's disappointment, she didn't react. Instead, she leaned out suddenly, cupping a hand around her ear.

"Did you hear that, Bee?"

But of course, Bee hadn't heard a thing.

"It's the Cricket Communications Network. The F.L.E.A. needs us." She made big buggy eyes at Bee. "Are you up to the task?"

"Well ..." Bee looked down at her new badge again. It *was* quite shiny. And sub-agent in training? It wasn't *that* bad for her first day on the job. She supposed she still had a lot to learn about the miniature world, and Flea might be just the parasite to teach her.

"Well ..." she said again, but this time she was pausing only for effect. "You know what they say:

Whenever there's trouble, F.L.E.A.'s there on the double."

Flea leapt onto Bee's back and threw her claws up in the air. "Yeehaw! Off we go!"

Bee didn't budge.

"Giddyup!" Flea banged her heels against Bee's sides.

"Aren't you forgetting something?" Bee asked out of the side of her mouth.

"Huh?" Flea scrunched up her mouthparts. "Oh!" she said. "Giddyup, *please*!"

Bee couldn't help smiling. It *was* an improvement. "I actually meant the sirens," she said.

"Oh! Obviously!" Flea said. "I was just waiting."

"Waiting for what?"

"For you to join in. That is, if you think you can be LOUD ENOUGH. Do you think you can be loud enough, Bee?"

"I'll do my best, Flea!"

"What's that?" Flea cupped a hand around her ear.

"I'LL DO MY BEST, FLEA!" Bee shouted.

"Much better."

Then Flea grabbed hold of Bee's antennae, and they both began to wail together:

"WEEE-OOOOO! WEEE-OOOOO! WEEE-OOOOO!"

THE END

Have you got what it
takes to be an official
F.L.E.A. agent?

Take this teeny-tiny
test to find out!

Fleas do drink blood,

but they don't wear fanny packs. And bees like to keep busy, but they aren't great spellers. In the same way, some of the other things Bee and Flea encounter in the book are partly real and partly made up.

In each of the following, there are three facts and one falsehood. Can you sort out fact from fiction to earn your official F.L.E.A. badge?

Circle the one statement you think is FALSE, then check your results on the next page.

1. Compost heaps are piles of organic waste (like wilted lettuce and black banana peels) that decompose, or rot, to produce soil. They are...

a) filled with trillions of tiny life-forms

b) usually very smelly

c) reliant on the help of different types of worms to keep them healthy

d) contaminated by things like plastic, little stickers on fruit and vegetable peels, and bones from meat

2. Potworms and nematodes are types of small, white thread-like worms that can live in compost. These critters...

a) help get air into the soil by tunneling to loosen it up

b) eat decaying organic matter, like fruit and veggie peels

c) love to accessorize—for example, by
   wearing tiny bow ties

d) are sometimes mistaken for one another
   (though potworms are bigger and
   sometimes eat nematodes!)

**3. Woodlice (also called potato bugs,
chuggy pigs, and chisel hogs) are small
armor-plated insects that tend to live
in decomposing wood. They...**

a) are related to crustaceans, like shrimp
   and crabs

b) eat decaying wood, leaf litter, fungi,
   and even their own poop

c) can roll themselves up into a ball for
   protection

d) like to play a party game where they
   smack each other on the head with
   a stick

4. Compost rotifers are part of the pseudocoelomate (say: soo-doe-SEE-lo-mate) family. They are known to ...

a) live in soil, water, and moss

b) enjoy chatting about their meals with anyone who asks

c) eat pretty much all day long

d) be too tiny to be seen except under a microscope

5. Bacteria are single-celled organisms that are the oldest known life-form on the planet. They ...

a) are great dancers

b) come in all sorts of shapes, including rods, spirals, and spheres

c) generally aren't dangerous to humans, although some can make us sick

d) break down organic matter in compost by eating and digesting it

6. **Mites are tiny eight-legged insects that live in soil, in water, and even on people! These mini-beasties ...**

a) are related to spiders

b) poop pretty much everywhere

c) come in a variety of colors, like brown, white, clear, and red

d) are very talented at dodge-poop

If you got between **four and six** right: Good job! Wear your F.L.E.A. badge with pride!

Make your own badge by tracing this shape onto a piece of blank paper and cutting it out!

If you got **three or fewer** right: Nice try! Why not give the quiz another shot to move up from sub-agent to full agent? I've got a *flea*-ling you can do it if you just *bee*-lieve in yourself!